Is Anyb

written by Jack Gabolinscy
illustrated by Anthony Elworthy

Theo was thirteen years old and a total space freak. He loved
astronomy. His nose was forever buried in books about black
holes; his mind exploring the internet for information about the
parallel universe; or his vivid imagination conjuring up visions of
extra-terrestrial beings.

He was convinced that one day he would be the first human being
to contact intelligent life in the outer cosmos.

He had attempted, unsuccessfully, to communicate numerous
times before, but today, he was confident, would be different.

Today he would make contact with an alien, and in doing so write
his name in the history books alongside Albert Einstein, Neil
Armstrong and Elvis Presley.

3

He typed the address:

sww@allgalaxiesandblackholesintheuniverse

Then he typed the message:

"Hello. Hello. Hello. Is anybody out there? This is Theo Greenhelg Whittier from Planet Earth. If you receive this message and want to be friends please reply. Theo"

He checked and double-checked, crossed his fingers (and his eyes for good luck), then hit SEND.

4

The battered old computer wound up like a supersonic jet. The microwave oven that he'd connected to generate extra energy pulsed purple and pink; the desk shook; the ceiling fan spun a force 10 cyclone; paper scraps and dirty socks flew around the room. Unperturbed, Theo smiled, turned up the volume and increased the microwave power to maximum.

He stacked two heavy piles of books onto the desk to reduce the vibration, then sat patiently watching the transmission signal beaming his historic message out through the World Wide Web, across the Milky Way, and deep into the immensity of the Space Wide Web. "Is anybody out there?" he asked himself, though he never doubted there was. "How long will it take? Minutes? Hours? Days?"

Hello Is anybody out there?

Sai Wala Walakar, Theo's best friend, happened to live next door. He was stepping out of his back door on the way to visit Theo when his phone alerted him to an incoming email message. He opened it and read:

"Hello. Hello. Hello. Is anybody out there? This is Theo Greenhelg Whittier from Earth. If you receive this message and want to be friends please reply. Theo"

Sai thought Theo was being funny. He was accustomed to his crazy tricks, so he laughed and played along with the joke. ***"Hello. Hello. Hello Theo."*** He typed his reply as he reached Theo's back door. ***"Yes, I am out here. I want to be friends with you Theo. SWW"*** He abbreviated his signature as usual, using only his initials to save words, depressed SEND then waited for Theo to open the door.

Theo went into orbit when he read Sai's message. He saw the SWW signature and was totally convinced it had come from some distant planet on the Space Wide Web. He was so excited that he could barely control his trembling fingers to type a reply:

"Hello SWW. I am pleased to talk to you. I have always wanted to communicate with an extra-terrestrial being, but now that you have appeared I don't know what to say."

14

"You could start by opening your back door and letting me in," replied Sai.

Theo couldn't believe it. Not only did the alien want to communicate, it also wanted to visit!

"Are you sure?" he asked. *"Don't you think we should talk and become better acquainted before we meet?"*

"Don't be an idiot," answered Sai. *"You've had your joke. Now open the door and let me in, or I'll huff and I'll puff and I'll blow your door down."* He knocked loudly to show his impatience.

16

Theo read the new message at the same time as he heard the violent thumping on the door, and thought the alien was trying to break in. He imagined a gigantic wolf-like monster (with scales instead of fur) lurking on the doorstep, waiting for him to open the door.

"No. No. I've changed my mind," he replied in a panic.
"I don't want to communicate after all. I'm sorry you made such a long voyage for nothing, but go back home now. Please."

Sai could tell that Theo was upset, but he didn't understand why. **"Calm down Theo,"** he wrote. **"You're over-excited. You're panicking for no good reason. This is me, Sai. I've only come from next door. My mother has cooked us a bowl of delicious curried chicken and rice for dinner. Do you really want me to take it back home?"**

Theo was unconvinced. **"I don't believe you,"** he replied. **"You're trying to trick me into letting you in so you can capture and devour me."**

20

Sai lifted the lid from the curry bowl, allowing the spicy aroma of curried chicken and vegetables to waft in through the keyhole. "Is that the smell of an evil alien, or is that my mother's cooking?" he called. Instantly Theo's mouth watered as he smelt Mrs Walakas' delicious curry.

"Why didn't you say that in the first place?" he growled, almost tearing the door off its hinges in his haste to get to the food.

Two minutes later they were back in Theo's room enjoying their dinner. The computer beeped.

Theo opened the new e-mail and read aloud:

"Hello. Hello. Hello. I want to be friends with you. I am Hocus Pocus from the planet Crocus in the outer SWW. Will you be my friend?"

Theo reread the message suspiciously. His last experience had taught him to be cautious about aliens from outer space. "What do you think?" he asked Sai. "Should I reply?"

"It's up to you," smiled his friend, sneaking his phone back into his pocket. "What do *you* think?"